little peep

by jack kent

Simon and Schuster Books for Young Readers
Published by Simon & Schuster Inc.,
New York

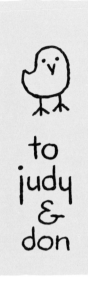

to
judy
&
don

Simon and Schuster Books for Young Readers
Simon & Schuster Building
Rockefeller Center
1230 Avenue of the Americas
New York, New York 10020

Library of Congress Cat. in Pub. Data—
Kent, Jack.   Little Peep.
SUMMARY: A chick is warned by the other barnyard
animals never to annoy the old rooster, because without
him to bring up the sun, there may be no future.
[1. Domestic animals—Fiction] I. Title. PZ7.K414Li
[E]   80-26015
ISBN 0-671-67051-4
ISBN 0-671-67052-2 (pbk)

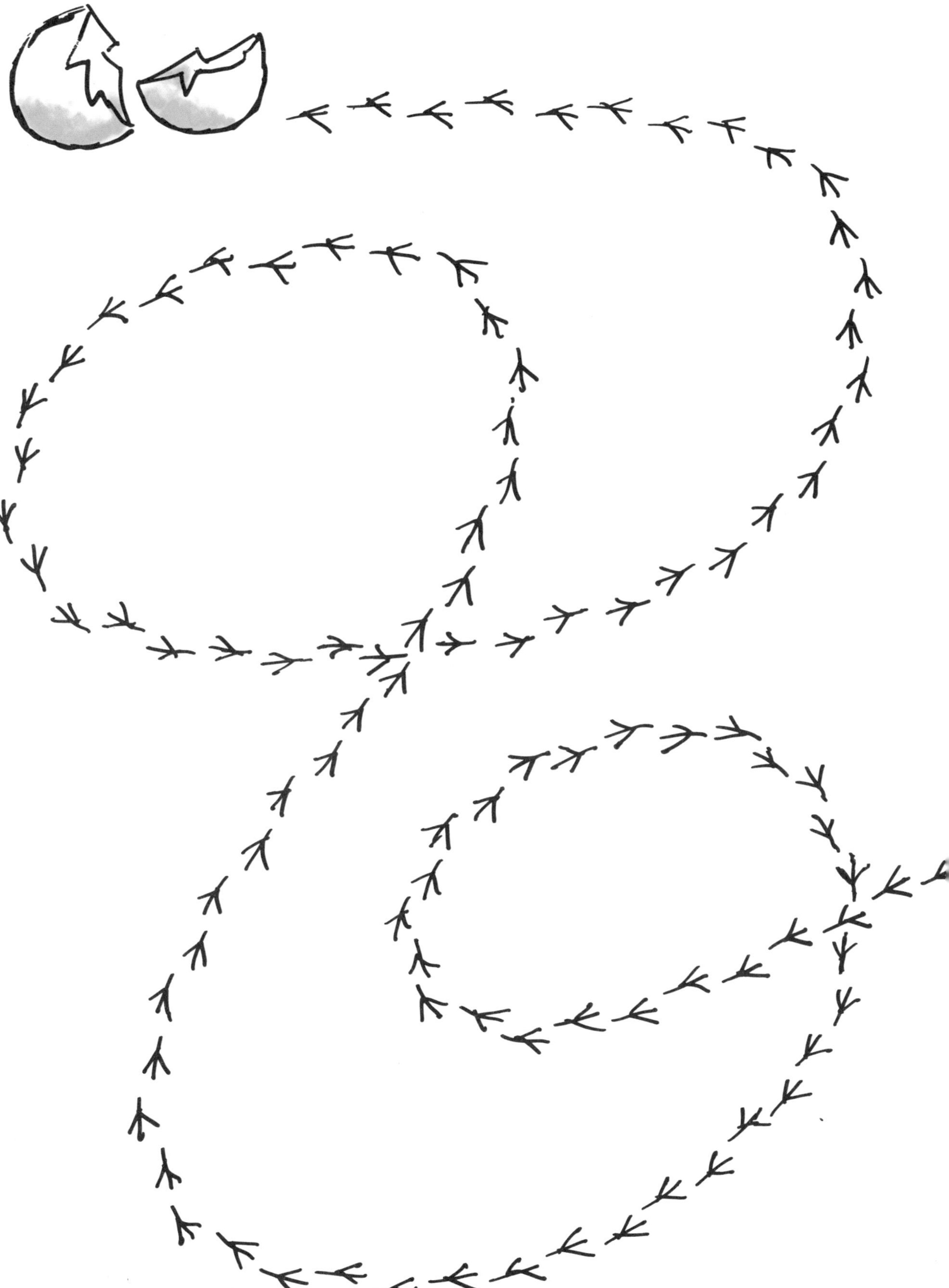

"Cock-a-doodle-doo!"

What was that?

"Cock-a-doodle-doo!"

There it was again!
It was the grandest sound
Little Peep had ever heard.
But then he hadn't heard
very many. He had only
just been hatched.

"Cock-a-doodle-doo!"
The cock was perched
atop the pump, crowing
to the dawn.

The sun came up. The animals yawned and stretched and began bustling about the barnyard, looking for breakfast.

The cock strutted back and forth, acting very important. "Get out of my way, horse!" The horse got out of the cock's way.

"Stand aside, cow!"
The cow stood aside.

"You're in my path, goat!"
The goat moved out of the cock's path.

"Give that to me, pig!" The pig gave the cock the
ear of corn he had been nibbling on.

"I only want the kernels," said the cock, pecking
at the corn. "You may have the cob when I'm through."
The pig looked grateful.

A small bit of corn fell to
one side and Little Peep ate it.

"Who is this person?"
demanded the cock angrily.
"Remove him at once!"

The animals rushed over and shooed Little Peep to the other side of the barnyard.

"You must be new here," said the pig.

"I am," Little Peep admitted. "I was just hatched."

"That's why you didn't know any better," said the goat.

"You could have gotten us into a lot of trouble," said the cow.

"You must never never never annoy the cock," said the horse.

"Never never never," they all said together.

"Why?" asked Little Peep.

"Because he might get huffy and refuse to crow,"
said the pig.

"When the cock crows the sun comes up,"
said the goat.

"And if he didn't it wouldn't," said the horse.

"And then it would be night all day," said the cow,
"and there wouldn't be any tomorrow tomorrow."

"So never never never annoy the cock," they said.
"Never never never!"

All day long the cock went strutting about, telling everybody what to do and how to do it.

Little Peep watched and thought what fun it must be to be that sassy and get away with it. He wanted to be like the cock.

"And why not?" he thought to himself. "What's so great about cock-a-doodle-doo? I'll bet I could do it myself."

He decided to try.

That night, when all of the animals were asleep, Little Peep went to the pump. It was awfully high.

But there was a bucket next to it. Little Peep hopped up onto the handle of the bucket and then onto the rim. From there he hopped onto the pump's spout. Then he hopped onto the lip of a tin cup that was balanced on the spout. And that was as high as Little Peep could go. "It's high enough," he decided.

Little Peep threw back his head
and crowed. "Peep-a-deedle-peep!"
It seemed to lack something, somehow.

Little Peep tried again, louder
this time. "PEEP-A-DEEDLE-PEEP!"

Little Peep couldn't understand it.
"It sounds all right in my head,
but it comes out all wrong," he said.

He took a deep breath and tried
again. "Peep-a-DOODLE-peep!"
His voice was changing.

It surprised Little Peep and made
him jump. He lost his balance and
fell head first into the tin cup.

In trying to right himself,
Little Peep jostled the cup
and it fell off the spout.
Little Peep and the cup
tumbled into the bucket
with a clatter that made the
dog at the farmhouse bark.

"Wake up, Henry!" said the
farmer's wife. "There's something
wrong in the barnyard!"

The farmer got up and switched on the floodlight. It lit up the barnyard bright as day.

The animals yawned and stretched and began bustling about the barnyard, looking for breakfast.

The cock was confused. "How can it be morning if I haven't crowed?" he said to himself. He pecked at an ear of corn and wondered about it.

The farmer came into the barnyard.
He was in his pajamas and he carried a gun.
But he couldn't find anything wrong,
except that all of the animals were awake.

"What are you doing up in the middle of
the night?" the farmer asked the animals.
"Go back to sleep!"

And he went back to the farmhouse.

"The middle of the night?" said the cow in surprise. "Why is it daylight in the middle of the night?"

All of the animals turned and stared at the cock.

"Don't look at me," said the cock. "It isn't my doing."

"*I* did it,"
said the bucket
by the pump.

The cow looked into the bucket
and saw Little Peep.
"How could YOU have done it?"
she asked, tipping the bucket
over so Little Peep could
get out. "The cock is the only
one who can make the sun
come up. He says so himself."

"But the cock said he DIDN'T do it THIS time,"
the pig reminded her.

All the animals turned and stared at the cock again.

The cock fidgeted nervously. "It's true,"
he admitted, "I didn't crow."

"*I* did it," said Little Peep.
"MY crowing made the sun come up."
He strutted over to where the cock
was. "Get out of my way, cock!"
Little Peep said. "You're in my
path!"

"Now see here...!" the cock began.

But just then the farmer
switched off the floodlight.
The barnyard was dark again.

All of the animals went back to sleep.
All except the cock and Little Peep.
They stayed awake and argued.

"If I HAD crowed," said the cock, "the daylight would have lasted longer than THAT!"

"Well, it was my very first try," Little Peep said. "I'll do better with practice."

"And besides," said the cock, "I wouldn't have been so stupid as to make the sun come up in the middle of the night."

"I can't tell time yet," Little Peep said.
"I can't learn everything all at once."

They argued and they fussed and
they fussed and they argued. They
were still arguing when dawn came.

The animals yawned and stretched and began bustling about the barnyard, looking for breakfast.

"Well, which one of you made the sun come up THIS time?" asked the cow.

The cock stared at the sun in surprise. "I hadn't even noticed it was up!" he said.

"Neither had I," said Little Peep.

"You mean neither one of you crowed, but the sun
came up ANYWAY?" said the horse.

"I think I understand," said the goat.
"The sun doesn't come up because the cock crows,
the cock crows because the sun comes up."

"Pooh!" said the cow.
"ANYBODY can do THAT!

MOO-KA-DOODLE-MOO!"
she crowed, and giggled.

"OINK-A-DIDDLE-OINK!"
crowed the pig.

The horse and the goat
laughed so hard they had
to hold each other up.

They strutted over to the cock and Little Peep.
"Get out of the way!" they said. "You're standing
in our path!"